RAMU and CHENNAI

Brothers of the Wild

RAMU and CHENNAI

Brothers of the Wild

by Dr. Michael Fox

illustrated by Michael Hampshire

Coward, McCann & Geoghegan, Inc.

New York

Acknowledgments

The author is grateful for the inspiration of the wild life he encountered while .studying the behavior and ecology of the Chennai or Whistling Jungle Dog in the jungle of South West India. He is also appreciative of the advice and help of his research assistant, Mr. A. J. T. John Singh, and is especially grateful for the hospitality and observations of Mr. E. R. C. Davidar who has spent many years studying the natural history of this fascinating part of our world.

SBN: GB-698-30591-4
SBN: TR-698-20338-0

Library of Congress Catalog Card Number: 75-10453

Printed in the United States of America
08214

For my brothers' children
and for mine,
Wylie and Camilla.

CONTENTS

RAMU and CHENNAI

Brothers of the Wild

The jungle is a peculiar organism of unlimited kindness and benevolence that makes no demands for its sustenance and extends generously the products of its life activity, it affords protection to all beings, offering shade even to the axe man who destroys it.

—GAUTAMA BUDDHA

1 The World of the Jungle

Cradled between the Nilgiris, or Blue Hills, of South West India lies a long, wide jungle valley. From these high hills, the valley looks like a restful quilt of greens and browns embroidered with brighter threads of green and gold that trace the courses of meandering rivers. It is early afternoon and most of the jungle creatures are resting. Only the birds sing and flit under the shade of the trees.

The valley seems inviting, but it is no place for people to sleep. If you mind your own business, avoid poking around in the underbrush where a viper may be resting, and keep a watchful eye out for the elephants browsing in tall bamboo by the rivers, no harm will come to you.

But no matter how quietly you move, the ever-present birds will give you away, sounding off alarm calls that alert their companions and the other animals nearby. If you hide motionless in the shadows for a while, the birds will start singing again. From a nearby tree, though, a large gray langur monkey, acting as a sentry or lookout for his family, may have his eye on you. A couple of hoots from him will awaken half the jungle. If only you could be invisible, you could move safely, without frightening anyone.

There is one man who is almost invisible. He lives in a small clearing in the jungle with his relatives. Because Sikka Bunda knows the jungle so well, he is a Shikari, one who guides hunters and naturalists where alone they would see nothing, easily get lost, and possibly die. Sikka Bunda teaches his twelve-year-old son, Ramu, the secrets of the jungle. Ramu knows what the calls of many of the birds mean. He recognizes the chattering that jungle babblers make when they are alarmed by a chennai, the wild dog of India. He knows the *ca-caw* of a jungle crow who has found a dead animal to feast on. He knows, too, that the trumpeting of the deer and the squawk of jungle fowl and peacocks mean danger. Often there are false alarms. Deer, cautiously drinking in the open, may hear the alarm cry of the malabar squirrel and dash for cover. The squirrel may only have been swearing at a troop of monkeys. But if the squirrel was alarmed by a passing leopard, its cry gives the deer a fair, but unintentional, chance to escape.

Ramu has learned his way along countless game trails, those narrow paths worn into the earth over hundreds of years by passing deer as they move from one browsing area to another. Other animals use these trails too: porcupines, mongooses, leopards, elephants and chennai. Ramu knows who passed by most recently because he can read the tracks that the animal's feet made in the soft red dust.

When he goes exploring by himself, he carries an old aruval (pronounced *aruwal*). This is the knife his grandfather, who was once a famous Shikari, gave him before he became a village elder. When Ramu sets out alone, he tells his parents the direction he will follow—just in case of trouble. He keeps a mental note of the position of the sun, using this to check the time of day and direction. Whenever possible he walks with the breeze blow-

ing in his face so that the animals ahead will be less likely to smell or hear him. As he approaches a bend in the trail, he goes slowly and cautiously looks around the bend so that he will be able to spot whatever animal might be there, before it sees him. He wears soft leather sandals to protect his feet from stones and thorns, and a patched old khaki army shirt for camouflage.

If a deer sees him, Ramu freezes—even in mid-stride. He does not budge an inch until the animal begins to browse again. Then he steps forward a few paces and stops again as the animal looks at him once more. This way he is able to get very close, close enough to almost touch them. Close up, Ramu can hear the mewing, chattering noises they make to each other—warm, friendly sounds quite different from their alarm trumpet. Ramu has imitated these sounds. When he does the deer usually become calm, and he is able to watch them.

Ramu has learned to be patient and sit for hours in a hide made of thornbushes or perched high up in a leafy tree. In this way he can watch monkeys picking their day-long meals out of the trees, breaking off now and again to groom each other or play. Gradually he has learned the language of these animals and the way they communicate by using various body postures and facial expressions.

During his explorations, Ramu has come to recognize certain individuals.

Some are shy and timid, others bold and headstrong, with a bent for mischief, be they deer, wild dogs, or monkeys. And there is always a leader, a chain of command, and a family structure of mothers, fathers, children, aunts, uncles, and even grandparents.

Often Ramu would go out into the jungle with his father, Sikka Bunda. On special rare occasions he would join a hunting party and help carry the supplies. Ramu was surprised by how little many of these people knew about the ways of the jungle. He was proud of his father who knew so much more than these wealthy visitors from England, America, and other foreign lands.

2 The Jungle People

Ramu's grandfather, Siddah, taught him that God was everywhere—in the trees, the rivers, in deer, birds, and everything that lives and dies. Siddah said that heaven was on earth and not someplace in the sky.

Ramu found this idea difficult to accept when he found the remains of a deer torn apart by a leopard or saw the poverty and sickness in the big city of Bangalore. But when he was alone in the jungle, he did feel that he was part of something wonderful. He could accept the fact that the leopards and the wild dogs had to kill to live.

Ramu's people were very much part of the jungle. They grazed their cattle, goats, and sheep there. Surprisingly few were killed by leopards or wild dogs, even though the livestock was usually unguarded during the day. At night they were herded together in enclosures made of tree branches, bamboo, and interwoven thornbushes. Sometimes a leopard will get inside and kill one of the calves, but this is rare. A leopard knows it could be crushed by the enraged and fearful cattle. Sheep and goats are easier prey. Many nights Ramu and his friends stand guard, armed with stones and old tin cans to beat and frighten away a leopard that is known to have moved into the area.

On some of the pattis, or farms, they used poison to kill such marauders. Filling a dead calf with poison and leaving it out as bait, the farmers had killed many leopards and wild dogs. Other animals that eat the carrion, or remains, such as porcupines, jackals, jungle crows and vultures, and hyenas and wildcats were also killed. And many of the farmer's dogs had been poisoned too. By the time Ramu was ten, not a single tiger, the worst poacher of the farmers' livestock, was to be found in his valley. But he remembers well the tiger's roar at night, and its beauty, stealth, and strength.

Ramu realized that he and his people wanted to live peacefully with the wild animals and share the jungle with them, and he was glad that his relatives, thanks to his grandfather's wisdom, no longer used poison. "You will kill every animal in the jungle except the one you are after if you use a poisoned bait," his grandfather used to say. But some of their neighbors still used poison, even though it was no way to stop the wild dogs from killing.

By far the worst character to come out of the jungle was the rogue elephant, Ramu thought. Just for fun—or out of sheer cussedness—an elephant would tear half the roof off a cottage or mash a field of potatoes into a pulp. When the people came out, shouted at him, and threw stones and firecrackers to shoo him away, he might lose his temper and go on a rampage, knocking down fences, squashing cottages as though they were dolls' houses, and even maiming and killing some of the less agile villagers. More than one person had fainted on the spot or become paralyzed with fear and unable to run when confronted by the terrifying trumpeting scream of an elephant. The elephant was often just as surprised and scared as they, and may have been trumpeting in fear.

One night a big tusker came into Ramu's patti

and woke everyone up with an earthshaking bel-
low. Peeping out the window, Ramu saw this
tusker idly walking around in the bright moonlight,
looking for some mischief. Out of the shadows of
a large banyan tree came a young domestic bull
buffalo, with his nose high in the air in a threaten-
ing gesture. Few animals would dare tangle with
a bull buffalo who, with his enormous horns, guards
his herd from all danger. Ramu remembered see-

ing a domestic buffalo drive a *tiger* away from a young calf and he watched this encounter with interest.

The buffalo slowly and steadily walked straight toward the elephant, and then stopped, snorted, and scraped the ground with his front feet. Was he going to charge at the elephant, Ramu wondered. Suddenly the elephant swung around, raised his trunk high, and flapped his great ears. The buffalo reared up and charged. But the charge stopped a few feet from the tusker, who waved his trunk at the buffalo's horns before backing off and lowering his ears. Then the elephant turned and ran, with the buffalo chasing him. Each time the elephant stopped and turned to face him, the buffalo would make a halfhearted charge.

Ramu deduced that they were playing. His father said that he was quite right and told him, for perhaps the hundredth time, of the day when he saw a langur monkey riding on the back of a deer. Many different animals of the jungle look out for one another. They often have friendly relationships. Mongooses and porcupines may live peacefully in the denning area where the cubs of chennai are raised. Farm, or "pie," dogs may be accepted into a chennai pack and go hunting with them. The small spotted deer, or chitae, will often herd and graze and even play with the giant deer, or sambhur. All the deer readily accept the drongo bird on their backs. This bird can mimic the sounds of just about any animal in the jungle. The drongo picks ticks and fleas off the deer; in return for his services, the bird gets a free dinner of ticks and fleas!

Elephants provide a good service to the other animals of the jungle. In a way they are super game wardens because their presence in the jungle keeps away many would-be poachers and sandalwood smugglers who are fearful of elephants and think they're all man-killers.

The sandalwood smugglers are people who illegally cut down sandalwood trees and hack out the inner core of the tree from which precious sandalwood oil is extracted. Because these men are so greedy, they will cut down even small trees, and the forest department was worried that there would soon be no sandalwood trees left, except perhaps in the most remote parts of the jungle. Anyone caught smuggling sandalwood, because it was now rare and almost as precious as gold, would be put into prison. But the jungle is just too large for the forest guards to cover, and many such beautiful trees are needlessly destroyed by these thieves.

For thousands of years Ramu's people have been collecting riches from the jungle, without destroying it in the process. Creeping vines, such as lianas, serve as rope or wire. Once every forty or more years the bamboo bursts into flower; it will shortly die. Bamboo seeds develop in the flowers, and parakeets, monkeys, and jungle fowl feast upon it before villagers come to shake down the nutritious rice for themselves. The cut trunks of bamboo are used to make cups and containers. Nutmeg, wild honey, soap nuts to make into soap, lichens for making dyes, tamarind fruit that they dry and grind for use as a condiment, and many medicinal plants are collected and sold. Knowing which plants, where they are, and what time of the year to pick them is all part of growing up in the jungle.

Much of the year is dry and hot in this valley of the Nilgiris. October and November is the rainy season. Then the rivers roar and the dry gullies, or nallahs, are full. Flowers of every color and kind burst into bloom. Millions of insects emerge. Some are so small you can hardly see them, but you know they are there because they buzz and sometimes bite. Others are bigger than your fist and may be more brightly colored than the flowers themselves. This is the time when the jungle bears its

25

fruit. The trees and shrubs ripen, and most of the animals have their young. The timing is just right because there will be plenty of food in the jungle to provide the mothers and their growing offspring with food. Hundreds of fawns are born to the deer, and around the same time the deer's predators also bear their young. The deer produce more fawns than the land could possibly support, and some of these fawns, together with less swift or aged adults, are taken by such predators as the leopard and wild dog.

Soon after this rainy season the greatest adventure in Ramu's life began.

3 A Discovery

It was Saturday, Ramu's favorite day because there was no school and because on Saturdays his younger sister, Indhrani, did his chores for him. This meant cleaning out the cooking pots and helping his mother carry water and firewood for the stove on which she cooked all their meals. He called to his pet crow, Baswey. She flew right to him from her roost on the cottage roof, and he threw her a few pieces of dried fish. She cawed gratefully but hopped just out of reach when he held out his hand. She was attached to Ramu because he had rescued her as a fledgling from the jaws of a wildcat, but, like most birds, she never liked to be touched. After bathing in the nearby river and brushing his teeth with a piece of banyan tree root, Ramu pulled out his worn knapsack and his aruval. He was going into the jungle for the day. He wrapped up some pieces of papaya fruit in a square of palm leaf and stuffed some chappatis (a kind of flat bread pancake) into the sack. Then, laying his knapsack and aruval on the doorstep, he ran in and filled his canteen with water. When he got outside, the knapsack was gone.

He looked around puzzled, and went back indoors. No, he hadn't left it by the water can; where was it? Looking outside again, he saw Guda, his mischievous billy goat, dragging the knapsack by the strap. Guda was heading straight for the river! The goat had done this kind of thing before. Once he ran off with a whole basket of chillies, or hot peppers. Ramu's mother stood back and let Guda taste them, hoping to cure the goat once and for all of being a playful nuisance. Chillies are very hot, and these were the hottest variety. But Guda polished off all the chillies in two wags of his cheeky tail. Then he started to eat the straw basket.

Ramu took an empty rifle cartridge case from his pocket and gave three toots. It worked! Guda dropped the knapsack by the edge of the river, spilling chappatis all over the ground. Looking surprised, he turned in the direction of the sound. Seeing that it was only Ramu, his master, Guda tried to grab one of the chappatis. But by then Ramu had the goat by the tail and was dragging him away. Guda lost this round, but with his head high in the air and his tail up, he trotted proudly back to his companions, bleating squeakily with every other step.

Ramu was delighted that his trick had worked. Mr. David, who often visited the valley to study the animals, had given him the cartridge. He told Ramu that three or four toots on it might call up some wild dogs, since they make a similar tooting when they are rallying together. Other animals that fear the wild dog may panic on hearing this call. It worked this way with Guda. *Perhaps,* thought Ramu as he packed his knapsack again, *I could call the wild dogs with it. Wouldn't it be nice,* he imagined, *to have a different kind of whistle for each animal of the jungle.*

These thoughts carried him over the hill behind his house. He was walking east in an easy but cautious pace. He had decided to explore a part of the jungle where he had never been before. Because of the incident with Guda, he had forgotten to tell his parents where he was going. Ramu followed a game trail for about a mile along the top of the hills. The tracks on the trail told him that a leopard had walked along it for some distance the previous night, before turning off onto another trail. A nocturnal porcupine used the trail then too, preferring to scavenge for food at night. A few long quills made pencil lines in the dust because they dragged behind the animal as it ambled along. Here and there its tiny sausage-shaped droppings were evident. Ramu pressed one under his sandal. It was still soft: If the porcupine had passed the night before that, the droppings would have been baked hard by the sun. Ramu kicked the trail and the dust blew onto his leg. That was good. The breeze was in his face, and animals ahead of him would not catch his scent. They would be less likely to run off before he had a chance to see them.

By the time the sun was shining into his valley below (about seven A.M., Ramu calculated), he reached a big crossroads where the trail that led up from the valley intersected with one running along the edge of the hill. He rested there for a while, then pulled out his cartridge case and wondered if he should blow it. He saw that the tracks and many droppings of wild dogs were very fresh. They had probably trotted by an hour or two ahead of him. The tracks led up from a small valley on the other side of the hill and followed the ridge trail, continuing along the way he was going to take. *Off on their morning hunt*, Ramu concluded. *If I follow their tracks back to where they started, maybe I will find their den. It is probably somewhere down by the river on the other side of the hill—a good place to explore. I'd better watch out for the elephants in that bamboo by the river.*

So Ramu took the steep, rocky, and winding trail down the other side toward the river. He could hear the babel of countless animals in the valley. The hollow hoots of langur monkeys, the mewing catlike screams of peacocks, a malabar squirrel chattering like a machine gun. Far away, a stag gave his alarm toot to the rest of the herd: The wild dogs were probably stalking them. Halfway down the hill, a beautiful golden oriole, perched on a thornbush, caught his eye. Ramu took the next step without looking. He tripped and went head over heels almost on top of the bird. He had forgotten the rule of always looking at the trail for two paces ahead and *then* looking up.

Clumsy oaf, thought Ramu, *telling everyone*

below that I'm coming and sticking myself with thorns too. It hurts. He got up and pulled a dozen or more thorns out of his hands and shirt, before shouldering his knapsack. But where was his aruval? It must have flipped out of his hands into the bushes.

I can never lose that, he muttered to himself, desperately trying to poke around for it in the bushes.

Keep calm, a voice inside him said. With the sun behind him, he might catch the glint of the aruval blade. Ramu thought for a moment, looked up at the sun, then went up the trail a short distance and looked down. Rocks, thornbushes, white chips of quartz, prickly pear cactus—his keen eyes scanned every shape and shadow.

Relax. He commanded himself to be calm. *Let the knife come to you. Look down and walk across the hillside, and let the sun's reflection on the blade catch your eye.* This he did and he soon spotted something glinting half out of the shadow of a thornbush. He skipped down to find his precious aruval.

The thornbush was just on the edge of a very deep nallah, and looking down into the gully, he saw two large holes in the far side of the bank. The earth piled up outside them looked quite fresh. Something had been excavating a home there. Ramu ran back and got his knapsack. Then he stealthily climbed down into the gully.

It was cooler there and very quiet. Every stone he walked on seemed to shout, "Ouch—Ramu the curious is coming." He came near the first hole and bent down to look at the tracks in the soil. Wild dog.

It must be a wild dog's den. *I wonder if they left a guard or if they all go out hunting. Perhaps there's a mother with cubs in there and I should keep away,* he reasoned with himself. But curiosity got the better of him. Holding his aruval firmly in his right hand, he stuck his head into the hole and listened. Not a sound: no growls or whimpers. He listened even harder, and suddenly he felt a chill go up his back. Something was breathing inside the dark tunnel.

In fright he held his breath and strained his ears even more. The breathing stopped suddenly. Then Ramu realized it was his own breathing that was being magnified by the tunnel! He gave a sigh of relief and inspected the wild dog denning area more thoroughly. He found five big holes in all, four in the sides of the bank at various heights and one on the surface of the ground above the bank. Since not a sound came out of any of the holes, he decided to crawl inside and explore more thoroughly. From the inner pocket of his knapsack Ramu took a precious box of matches.

4 Wild Dog City

He crawled into the first and biggest hole; he lit a match and wriggled forward. By the light of the match he could see the tunnel disappearing ahead. How long it was—where would it lead to? Ramu squirmed forward a few more feet, pulling himself along by his elbows. It was hard going, but the air inside felt quite fresh and had not a trace of animal smell. Chennai are fastidious about keeping their denning areas spotlessly clean.

The tunnel grew wider and deeper, and Ramu realized he was in a den chamber where the cubs would lie. He was able to turn around, and he discovered that at the end of the chamber were two more tunnels. He took the one to his right. Just as his second match went out, he brushed something furry with his hand. It gave him the shivers. Ramu backed away as fast as he could into the main chamber. When he lit another match, he discovered that it was nothing more than a shred of deerskin the dogs had been playing with. Farther along this tunnel he found another fork, which had one branch leading him right back down into the first chamber. The other one led outside. Sitting inside the main chamber, he felt around in the soft earth. His hands told him that the hard things he kept touching were pieces of bone and teeth of some of the prey that earlier families of cubs must have chewed. He found something long and pointed, almost as thick as a pencil. A porcupine quill. He wondered how a wild dog could ever tackle a porcupine. Could a porcupine have lived here for a while when the chennai were not in residence? He took the tunnel on the left side of the main chamber and suddenly saw daylight. Ramu crawled out on top of the bank. "So that's three holes accounted for," he muttered. "Now for the other two." These, he discovered, were interconnected by another large chamber, the back of which linked up with the rest of the tunnels by a short, narrow passage.

It was indeed a wild dog city, he thought, as he finally crawled out. That labyrinth of tunnels must have taken years and years to tunnel out. "Ouch!" he cried. Something was biting his neck. He caught it and looked. To his surprise, it was a flea. Then he looked down at his shirt and found it covered with fleas! "I'm going to be eaten alive," Ramu moaned, as he methodically began to pick them off. How they held on—they must have been very hungry. *Perhaps the dogs haven't moved in yet,* he thought, *and haven't cleaned the place out thoroughly since they were last here.*

Ramu was so engrossed in de-fleaing himself in the quiet shade of a leafy tamarind tree that he didn't see the wild dogs coming down the nallah, and they didn't notice him—at first.

They came along in single file, trotting lightly over the boulders of the dry riverbed. They looked satisfied and relaxed after a successful morning hunt. Their deep-red coats flashed as they moved into patches of sunlight between the shadows of the trees and huge boulders along the bank. Their brown legs were almost invisible under the shadows of their bodies, so they seemed to glide easily with dark, bushy tails making jaunty streamers behind them.

Something made Ramu look up. Perhaps the energy they seemed to radiate made Ramu aware of something approaching. They moved so silently. Ramu froze, as yet unnoticed in the shadows of a tamarind tree. A flea bit hungrily into his earlobe, but he didn't move. *Wild dogs are coming*—his heart pounded and his legs began to shake. He wanted to run away. But Ramu's training took over. *Don't move,* said that voice so familiar to him. *If you run, they will chase you. Look around slowly for a safe place if you need it.* Just then the lead dog reached the "city." Immediately he picked up Ramu's scent. His excitement heralded the other dogs, and they ran around and in and out of the den, following Ramu's trail. There were eight dogs in all; two were leaner and lighter-colored than the others. *Probably last year's cubs,* Ramu thought. Three were a little smaller than the others and had very full tummies: Perhaps these were expectant mothers who would soon set up residence in the Wild Dog City and raise their cubs there.

While Ramu was watching the pack, he didn't notice one of the yearlings sniffing around the tamarind tree. Suddenly it saw him and, jumping back in surprise, let out a volley of yelping barks. In an instant, the dogs surrounded him on three sides.

His back was to the rocky bank. Ramu remembered how a deer looked after the wild dogs had finished it. Would that happen to him? Two of the males and one of the pregnant females growled and yikked at him, lunging forward then jumping back and then forward again. Each time they uttered a piercing yik. Ramu held his ground. He noticed that the younger dogs were looking at him rather curiously, while the other two females kept away from him, pacing anxiously to and fro. They were even more afraid than he. Longingly, he looked at his aruval lying in the dust by the dens. Having that in his hands would have made him feel a lot more comfortable.

Suddenly the dogs stopped barking and just stood or paced around in front of him. Now and then they uttered low growls. Clearly they were not out to kill him, and they seemed to be waiting for him to make the next move. Ramu knew they wanted him to leave their city, but how could he? They surrounded him on three sides and had him cornered against the steep, rocky bank. There was no way out. Only up. Ramu swiftly grabbed the lowest branch of the tamarind tree and hoisted himself. One by one the dogs came forward and sniffed where he had been standing, and then each looked

up at him in the tree. *What are they thinking?* he wondered. *They seem to be anxious to get rid of me, a stranger, but do not want to kill me.*

Then the dogs scattered in all directions, and moments later a familiar voice called out to him.

"Father, how did you know I was here?" asked Ramu.

"Oh, so you think you walk on air," replied his

father. "Did you hurt yourself badly when you tripped and fell into that thornbush?"

Ramu laughed. His father had tracked him, of course. Sometimes he could walk so quickly following the faintest tracks that Ramu swore that the wind or the stones spoke to his father. Grandfather Siddah said that if you lived long enough you would be able to talk to the stones and the

leaves, but Ramu could never tell when he was teasing or being serious. "Listen to the leaves and learn the language of the trees" was another of Siddah's favorite sayings.

"Come, give me your hand and let's be going home. You must be tired, and I'm sure you have an explanation for roosting up there. Did the dogs tree you?"

Ramu jumped into his outstretched arms and was glad to feel the strength and warmth of his father, and the familiar smell of the betel nut that his father liked to chew.

"You nearly knocked me over," exclaimed his father. "You'll soon be a man, but remember, part of growing up means being responsible and letting others know where you are going and. . . ."

The lecture continued until they were almost home, but his father's words just blew away like dust on an elephant's back. Ramu was too tired to listen. After supper, he felt revived enough to tell the rest of his family about his day.

"But the wild dogs may eat you if you go back there," his mother protested.

Ramu assured her that they didn't harm him but only tried to frighten him away from their city.

"Yes, he's quite right, right, the boy is quite

right," old Siddah chipped in. "The only thing that will kill a man is his own fear."

"Or a tiger, elephant, or sick man that people have driven crazy," added Ramu.

"Enough now," said his mother. "You are just spinning things along so you can stay up late—off to bed with you right now."

Just then Ramu remembered the fleas and told his mother.

"Any excuse to stay up late," she said in disbelief.

Rama moved closer then to the kerosene lamp and showed her one of the hungry black insects still clinging to his shirt. Two seconds later he was in the river and the whole family were making much fun of dipping him free of the fleas.

Ramu was soon asleep that night, but before his tired eyes closed, he made up his mind to go back the next day to Wild Dog City and find out more about those strange animals. Everyone said they were born killers, but they hadn't harmed him. What would one of them be like as a pet if he got it as a cub? And so he dreamed about having his own cub, which he called Chennai, meaning "red dog" in his language.

5 The Chennai

Ramu woke before the sun had risen over the hill. As he dressed, he remembered his dream, and ideas came to him—if he did get to know the wild dogs, perhaps he might get one—or if all of the adults were shot or poisoned he could get one—or . . . Ramu stopped. He knew there was no way he could get one out of that well-guarded city, and he would certainly never harm one of them in order to steal a cub. Grandfather Siddha had explored that dog city, and others, when he was a boy. But in his day there were only four holes. Now there were five. It certainly was an old city.

Suddenly a car horn blew and Ramu ran outside

to welcome his friend Mr. David who had come to pick up his father for a day's hunting. Although Mr. David was a very knowledgeable naturalist and loved every animal of the jungle, he would go shooting wild pigs, hare, pigeons, jungle fowl, and duck when there was a good surplus of such game. Unlike many hunters, he would never go out hunting if the surveys showed that there was not enough game. If he did, what would the rightful hunters—the leopards and chennai—do for food? "Everything has its place, and man must take second place to the hunters of the jungle," old Siddah would say. He approved of Mr. David. Both men appreciated the rights of animals and understood how the delicate balance of nature could be so easily upset by human beings.

A few years earlier, Mr. David's best bird dog, a red setter named Kipling, died horribly after nibbling on a dead calf. Some of the farmers had put out poisoned bait to kill a pair of wild dogs that had killed one of their cattle. Mr. David realized that the poison would also kill other innocent animals, and so he tried to talk the farmers out of using it. Few saw this his way, since the loss of one good cow was often half a poor man's fortune.

Usually the chennai don't bother domestic stock, clearly preferring the taste of wild animals. But very often the deer get one of the terrible diseases that the free-grazing domestic cattle infect them with, such as hoof-and-mouth disease and rinderpest. Whole herds of deer may be wiped out. In these years, many chennai starve to death or are forced to find another valley to hunt in because the deer population is low. A few chennai packs will stay on and kill the farmers' animals in order to survive.

This is not good for the chennai because the distemper disease that many farm dogs carry will infect them and kill most of them in a few weeks.

Mr. David was very worried about these problems. He wanted the best for the farmers and for the jungle animals alike. Things couldn't continue as they were. "Somewhere there must be an answer," he said to Ramu's father, while sipping a glass of sweet, milky tea. "I'm working on a report which I hope will set up some new guidelines for the farmers and for the forest department and the hunters as well. The wild animals must have better protection and a larger sanctuary that is properly managed."

Sikka Bunda nodded his head from side to side

46

—the Indian way of agreeing, which to us looks like a "no" of disapproval. "We need a large sanctuary for the wild animals and more trained people who know something about wildlife management," he replied.

The conversation continued for a while. Ramu enjoyed listening to Mr. David, for he would often learn something new. Mr. David coughed and straightened his hair, which he always did when he was ready to leave.

Sikka Bunda stood up and smiled at Ramu. "Yes, would you like to come with us today, young man?" Mr. David asked. He expected Ramu's whoop of joy, but instead Ramu asked about the chennai because . . . and in two seconds he told Mr. David of his adventure.

"Wait a minute," said Mr. David. "You really mean to say you actually went into the den? You are a plucky chap. And the dogs didn't attack you—now that confirms my suspicion that they are not bloody killers."

He then told Ramu about the ways of the chennai. "There are as many names for the red dog as there are different languages in our country. We, the Tamils, call him chennai, while the people up north refer to him as dhole. The dogs live in central and east Asia, as far north as Manchuria and Tibet, and as far south as here. They somehow got to the islands of Sumatra and Java, but never made it to Japan, Ceylon, or Borneo. A good name would be 'jungle whistling dog' since he's the only member of the dog family that can whistle and lives in the jungle." Mr. David paused while Ramu's mother gave him more tea.

Ramu was fidgety—he wanted to know what the cubs are like. Mr. David continued his lecture. "The chennai, who may hunt in packs of up to forty or more and have been known to kill tigers and leopards, will often raise several families of cubs in the same communal nursery."

This was Ramu's chance. "How can I get a cub to keep as a pet, and what are they like—would one make a good pet?" he asked, hoping Mr. David could help. Mr. David raised his bushy eyebrows right over the top of his glasses, which promptly slid down his nose.

Looking at Ramu's father, he said, "How do you think you would get along with a chennai cub, surrounded by farm stock and a community of people who don't like the chennai? He's a meat eater, too, and meat is very expensive."

"Best cross that river when you come to it,"

chuckled old Siddah, who was now sitting cross-legged on the floor next to the stove, grinding curry out of chillies, mustard seed, yellow turmeric, coriander, cinnamon, and other spices. Most of their meals consisted of rice, other grains, and a few vegetables, hotly spiced with curry. Meat was a rare luxury indeed.

"Well, are you coming with us, son?"

"No, thank you," replied Ramu. "I'm going to Wild Dog City again. This time I'm going to build a machan in that tamarind tree and watch them where they can't see me."

6 Inside the City

Ramu built his machan in the tree early that day, making a floor out of four thick trunks of bamboo, lashed down with vines between two branches. He hacked down shrubs with his aruval and draped them on the overhanging branches. Then he climbed into his cool, leafy hiding place and waited for the pack to return from their hunt.

He must have fallen asleep, for the next thing he remembered was feeling something pushing up hard against the bamboo floor of his machan. Ramu awoke with a start, terrified as to what monstrous thing it might be. He peered down. All that he could see was a dark gray mass with blotches of red dust on it. An elephant! Then he saw that its enormous tusks crossed each other in front of the trunk. It was the crossed tusker that two weeks earlier had crushed two villagers out tending their fields.

The elephant is trying to push me down, thought Ramu, holding on desperately to the thickest branch he could reach. Quite unexpectedly, the elephant ambled away, pausing to squirt some of the sand from the dry riverbed onto his back. Much of it showered into Ramu's hide. The elephant was only doing what elephants do—using a tree as a back scratcher!

Soon it was quiet again, and Ramu, much relieved, started to eat his chappatis. In the middle of a big bite, something on a branch just in front of him caught his eye. He never finished the bite, but froze with his mouth wide open. No need to frighten a little lizard by moving too quickly. The lizard, his color and complexion matching that of the bark of the tree and making him almost invisible, looked through one eye at Ramu. The lizard twisted his neck to get a better look and then darted away to snatch a caterpillar that was munching on a leaf. A green bee-eater, Ramu's favorite bird, flew into the

tree and perched right above his head. Then a coppersmith began its rhythmic song, just like a smith beating out a sheet of metal. *"Tam tam tam tad-tam tam tam tam-tad-tada tam tam tam."*

Suddenly both birds flew away. Had they seen Ramu? No, something else was coming. A malabar squirrel in a nearby tree was venting its alarm signal. A jungle fowl that had been scratching around in the bushes, making noises that sounded at first like one of the chennai, spluttered and squawked and ran for cover.

Ramu peered through the hide and saw the wild dogs coming down their usual rocky trail along the nallah. "One, two, three"—he counted them. There were only seven. One was missing, the fattest of the females. Had she been hurt on the hunt?

The dogs came into the denning area sniffing the ground carefully. One by one they worked their way over to the tamarind tree. They didn't even look up, much to Ramu's relief. The overpowering smell of the elephant must have covered his own scent. The itchy tusker had, at least, been a help to someone that day.

Quite unexpectedly, a dog came out of one of the den holes. It looked like the missing female, but it was no longer fat in the tummy and it was behaving just like a little puppy. With its tail low and wagging furiously, it scurried up to each of the other chennai, pushing against them with its body, then bowing down and poking them in the side of the mouth with its nose. It was whining and whimpering and furiously licking their lips at the same time. *What a performance,* exclaimed the surprised Ramu to himself. *It surely can't be the same dog.*

She persisted in this behavior until one of the

big males bent down and coughed up a large piece of meat for her, which she gobbled hungrily. The other two males and one of the yearlings also fed her. *Of course, she is a mother now and the others are feeding her,* Ramu deduced. He guessed, too, that she must now have a litter of cubs in one of the chambers that he was in only a day before. Just imagine! The other dogs would have a lot of hard work on their hands, for they would have to provide food for the other two females when their cubs were born.

The pack, one by one, ambled over to the leafy shade of a wild fig tree growing somehow between two enormous rocks. They settled down to rest. One of the yearlings chewed idly on a curved fork of deer antler, and its companion fell asleep, twitching now and again as it dreamed of hunting, of the smell of game, and perhaps even of its encounter the day before with Ramu. One of the distended females rolled on her side; it was much easier to rest that way. The other was panting a lot and kept looking at her sides. She would be the next to have cubs. One of the males half jumped into the air and snapped up a flying white ant or termite, a tasty treat. In this part of the world the termites build large cities that rise a few feet off the ground in large red mounds. Others coat the trunks of trees with the red earth and live underneath it. It's often difficult to tell a sitting chennai from one of these red termite mounds, and when one rests under a red-trunked tree, even a deer would have a job spotting it.

Ramu was getting very stiff from sitting so long in his machan. *I will have to get used to this if I'm going to watch these incredible animals and their cubs,* he thought. Their cubs. The day he saw them would be an exciting one.

Picking up his aruval and knapsack, Ramu carefully edged his way between the big fork in the tree and slid down. The wide trunk hid him from view. Luckily, the breeze rustling a stand of bamboo nearby created a perfect cover for his getaway. Silently, his feet touched the high bank of the nallah several feet above the riverbed and base of the tree where the dogs had trapped him. He crept softly away into the underbrush.

None of the dogs barked or chased him. He half expected the whole pack to be on his heels. This time he was lucky, but next time might not be so easy. When wild dogs have cubs, they are much more protective. They might attack him then. Worse still, he thought, his presence might disturb them to the point of abandoning their cubs or moving them to another denning area that he might never find. How careful he would have to be, since not all the dogs would be away hunting when he got there. Some would be nursing or guarding the cubs.

Ramu couldn't wait until the next weekend when he would return to Wild Dog City. At school his mind kept wandering back to the nallah and his hide in the tamarind tree. Instead of doing a geometry problem on his slate, he drew a neat outline of the interconnecting tunnels of the complex den. His teacher was not at all pleased and said that Pythagoras didn't crawl around in filthy dog dens when he was a boy. Ramu muttered that the dog dens were very clean and that he didn't want to be Pythagoras or any other kind of problem-knotting python, and that the most important thing for him right now was to learn more about the chennai.

His teacher gave Ramu extra homework that day for not being attentive in class. He had to work out how much earth the wild dogs removed to make one hundred feet of tunnel, three feet in diameter. He would allow for an extra twenty feet in his calculations to approximate the increased volume of the three chambers.

Some homework problem, but he couldn't grumble. With the help of his older cousin he eventually figured it out: 112,800 cubic feet of earth and since each cubic foot weighs about 100 pounds, the chennai must have dug out almost 42½ tons over the years!

7 Chases and Kills

His teacher was pleased with his work and decided to encourage Ramu more in his studies. "Sup-
pose you take Wednesday mornings off. You will
only be missing reading period and P. E. Prepare
a written report on your studies of the chennai and
read it to the class at the end of the term."

Ramu was delighted and whooped for joy, for-
getting to keep his voice down when speaking to
someone older. His teacher smiled and said, "Now
back to Pythagoras, young man."

Ramu had learned his lesson well. Without knowing anything of geometry he could never have

figured out just how much work the wild dog architects had done in making their city.

The next weekend he went back to the city. On the trail he came across the fresh tracks of several deer and wild dogs. The tracks dug hard into the ground and dust was kicked up around them—they were running hard. Soon after, Ramu heard the alarm trumpet of a spotted deer. Moments later a young stag, with eyes wide and ears laid back flat against its head, came racing across the trail. It was so panic-striken that it didn't even see him. Quickly Ramu crouched behind a bush. At that very instant the chennai appeared, hot on the deer's trail and yikking excitedly. The lead dog cut off and raced uphill; the others disappeared over a low rocky ridge.

Ramu waited for a while and suddenly the stag appeared again. Its mouth was wide open and its stumbling feet betrayed its exhaustion. The lead dog was only a few feet behind it. He had circled ahead of the stag and driven it back the way it had come. Ramu wondered why and he soon got the answer. Four other dogs appeared suddenly over the ridge and encircled their prey.

Ramu felt a little sick. The stag was a beautiful animal. Its soft pale-brown coat, flecked with spots of white like camouflage paint, would soon be torn by the chennai.

One of the dogs leaped at the stag's nose and held on. This seemed to paralyze the animal. The weight of the dog made it difficult for the stag to use its antlers. Nor could it easily strike out with its powerful front hooves. A chennai could be killed by a blow from a hard hoof or impaled by those sharp antlers. Swiftly, another dog bit into the

rump of the stag, and then the three other dogs were on it, tearing at its flanks. The deer went down, no longer kicking. It was in shock and felt no pain.

A crow who had been following the hunt began to *ca-caw* excitedly from the top of a nearby tree. Ramu was amazed at the speed with which the wild dogs ate the deer. Efficiently, they worked under the skin, freeing it so they could get at the tender meat

of the back, thighs, and shoulders. Within fifteen minutes they had finished. Half a dozen ravens had gathered, thanks to the rallying call of the first crow. Several vultures were circling overhead, and others were settling in the trees waiting their share of the wild dogs' kill. Soon the stag's bones would be picked clean. By the next morning, after the night-roaming jackals had finished, there would be nothing left but a few bones bleaching in the sun.

The lead dog was off first, calling the others to follow with a series of deep, short whistles. Obediently the other dogs ran to join him, uttering little whimpers as they hurried along. Ramu thought how different the whistling styles of various wild dogs were. Some had shrill whistles, others deep, some high and short. Occasionally Ramu even heard musical undulating whistles. *Surely,* thought Ramu, *each dog has its own style so the others could recognize its call.* Sometimes a dog might give several toots or just a few. A dog might whistle softly or give a volley of loud, insistent toots. Perhaps these calls had different meanings, like "Come, I am here" or "Where are you, I am here" or "I am here and here is food." No other dog in the world whistles: Most, like wolves, howl to communicate with one another over long distances.

Ramu decided that it was too late to go to Wild Dog City. The pack would return to feed the three mothers with cubs before he could get there. So he chose to follow a trail in a wide circle around their den, go along the river at the bottom of the valley, and then return home. On Sunday he would have to be out earlier.

About a mile from the Wild Dog City he came across a clearing where two trails intersected. There he found a familiar sight—dozens of wild dog droppings. Some were just ropes of matted hair from the fur swallowed by the dogs while eating their kill. Others were white, like thick chunks of chalk, from the soft bones the dogs had partially digested. *It's true,* he thought, *you can tell what a wild animal eats by looking at its droppings. You never have to see what it eats.* But why did the chennai always choose to deposit at these special spots? He wondered if they liked to do everything together, or whether this was some kind of signal to other packs that this was their hunting area. He would have to find out more about this from Mr. David.

He walked on a little farther and, coming upon a large mound of rocks, decided to eat his lunch. He chose a large flat rock to sit on. The other rocks around made it seem like a throne. "I am the maharaja of the Nilgiris," he pronounced, and nibbled regally on his chappati.

Unbeknown to Ramu, he was trespassing on someone else's throne. From the tall pillar of rock behind Ramu's back came an eighteen-inch tall mongoose, followed by his smaller mate. The mongoose stood up on a rock no more than ten feet away with his hair bristling and growled loudly at Ramu. His mate, more bashful, hid behind him. Ramu laughed softly and apologized. The mongooses went on their way, poking around in the rocks for food—insects, lizards, birds' eggs, and almost anything else they could find. Ramu remembered seeing a mongoose kill a deadly cobra once. The mongoose is quick and it has razor-sharp teeth.

Suddenly a rumpus started in a low tree a few yards away. Jungle babblers, also called Seven Sisters because they like to go around in groups, were chattering and flapping their wings wildly. Ramu couldn't see into the leafy tree too well, but he caught a quick movement of something brown dashing out of one tree and up a very tall eucalyptus tree next to it. Then a mongoose shot up the tree, growling. Were the two mongooses having a family argument? Then he heard a loud hiss and saw the striped head of a jungle cat. The mongooses had treed it! No doubt the wildcat, like Ramu, was a trespasser.

An hour later Ramu was down by the river. The trail led right to the water's edge and in the mud were footprints of many animals that had come to drink. He identified peacock, deer, porcupine, bear, and leopard tracks. The deer tracks were sometimes on top of the porcupine and leopard tracks. Ramu knew this meant that the deer had come later, probably early that morning, while the others had come to the river the night before. His teacher often said that Ramu could read tracks better than he could read books. Ramu remembered that he had Wednesday mornings off now, and he smiled happily.

A deep sigh from somewhere in the bamboo thicket made him jump. An elephant! Quickly he edged away, trying to walk silently on the crisp yellow leaves and twanging strands of bamboo branches that lay strewn on the ground. *Stupid,* he said to himself. *Should have noticed all that freshly torn bamboo lying around that the elephant had been eating.*

He felt the wind change, and the bamboo began to rustle ominously. The elephant was turning around as it caught Ramu's scent. It trumpeted and charged. Ramu ran for his life, zigzagging between the bushes. He expected at any moment to feel a hairy trunk around his waist or a heavy foot squashing him into the ground. He kept on running, only daring to look around when the crashing and pounding behind him had ceased. He had surprised a mother elephant and her baby, and she was being very protective of her youngster. Content that she had driven away the intruder, the elephant returned to her infant in the rustling shade of the bamboo.

The sound of cawing crows drew Ramu off the trail home to a clump of bushes. A jackal trotted away as ravens and vultures flapped noisily in the air. Under the bushes was a dead wild dog, headless and tailless. The sight angered and sickened Ramu. It was the work of a hunter who had shot the dog and removed its tail and head in order to claim the bounty of twenty rupees. He saw that the chennai had swollen teats. Somewhere some cubs would be hungry and calling for their mother. They would die unless another mother who happened to be sharing the same den was producing milk herself. Ramu felt that no animal should be outlawed and, like a wanted criminal, have a bounty on its head. In the old days, bounty hunters prospered on killing the chennai, for twenty rupees then was a lot of money. Fortunately, the bounty had not been increased. Twenty rupees was not worth as much today, and so the chennai had a better chance. Today only the odd hunter would bother trying to shoot them.

How many chennai are injured and die slowly, he thought as he turned for home. *How many are crippled forever by the hunters. These men must see the wild dogs as rivals or as merciless killers and kill them for these reasons—or for sport. The bounty isn't worth it.*

Ramu had collected a few more scratches in his wild flight from the elephant, and his khaki shirt was badly torn. His parents knew what must have happened as soon as he reached home.

"You really must be more careful, Ramu. You walk through the jungle as though it were your own fields," his mother said as she stitched up his shirt. Ramu felt that he knew the jungle better than his relatives' fields, but he kept his mouth shut. He had learned not to argue with his mother: He never won.

8 The Cubs Emerge

By sunrise the next day he was in his machan in the tamarind tree. He saw the dogs return from their hunt and feed the three mothers. The mothers came out of the city, whining, with lips pulled back, grinning just like human beings, and greeted the hunters. The hunters, in turn, fed the hungry mothers, then rested along the far bank of the nallah. Little else happened that day, but Ramu's patience was rewarded later in the afternoon. All the chennai came together in front of the city and, with tails wagging wildly, licked each other in a beautiful ceremony that Ramu realized was an expression of love. The two yearlings focused much of their attention on the lead male and one of the mothers. They were probably the yearlings' parents. The lead male was showered with the most affection. But there were no signs of jealousy or bossiness.

What kind and peace-loving animals they are, thought Ramu. *People just wouldn't believe how much the chennai care for each other. They just think they are all bloody killers.*

Suddenly the leader signalled and the dogs departed. The three mothers went back into the city. The pack was probably going off on a night hunt. Tonight would be the new moon, which the wild dogs seemed to favor. They would soon have to make more than one kill a day to feed the fast-growing cubs.

Ramu slipped undetected from his tree hide. He continued to visit the chennai whenever he could. Two weeks later, on a Wednesday morning, he had his first glimpse of what he had been hoping to see. A cub. He had been hearing growls and whines coming from the den, and it was clear that the cubs had to come out soon. He was half-dozing, thinking about what the cubs might be doing inside the den, when he saw something small and brown at the entrance of one of the tunnels.

He blinked and shook his head. Yes, it was a real chennai cub. Its watery eyes were accustomed to the darkness of the den, and it blinked in the strong sunlight. Sneezing unexpectedly, the cub lost its balance and rolled like a ball right down the steep slope of dirt that had been dug out of the tunnel. The cub let out a piercing yelp, and the five dogs resting along the nallah ran to its rescue. The yearlings were excited, gently pawing and licking the tiny cub as it tried to stand up. Because it was so round and fat, the cub was literally stuck on its back like a helpless turtle. Ramu covered his mouth, to stifle a giggle. Very gently, one of the males picked the cub up in his jaws and carried it, squirming, back into the den.

A deep growl echoed from inside the labyrinth and the male chennai backed out quickly. He was not yet welcome in the quarters of the protective mother. Moments later, though, she came out and wagged her tail and licked his face—as though to make things up. Then she faced the den hole and gave three gentle whistles. How and why she made that noise Ramu couldn't imagine. He soon found out.

70

The cubs came out of the den, one by one, blinking and wobbling on legs that were unsure in the bright, new world that exploded around them. Ramu could see differences in the cubs, even though they all had the same dusty brown color. Some came out boldly, sliding down the excavated "doorstep" without a squeak. Others came out hesitantly, calling out to their mother in whines and whimpers. She just sat there, rewarding each cub with many licks when they reached her.

The other dogs, too, fussed over the cubs. Every time they approached one of the cubs to sniff and kiss it, they would look apprehensively at the mother. Since she didn't growl disapprovingly at them, they had permission to muzzle the five cubs, with affection and curiosity.

The mother was still looking toward the den. Very slowly, a tiny cub, with one ear shredded by the chewing and sucking of bigger cubs, emerged. When the daylight hit his eyes, he stared back fiercely and growled. *What a brave little fellow,* thought Ramu. *He's a real chennai, even if he is the smallest.*

Ramu watched the cubs explore their new world. This was obviously their first time out of the den. A large rock was something to climb for one cub, something to sniff under for another. A long vine was something to taste for some, but one got caught in it and was frightened until it realized that vines don't bite. Ramu saw how each cub stepped hesitantly on sharp twigs and rocks. Their pads were not yet calloused like the adults. One of the larger cubs stumbled onto a big leaf and jumped back in surprise when the leaf crackled. It ventured forward, touching the leaf with its nose, and when it didn't move, the cub leaped at it. Just then a light breeze lifted the leaf over his head and the cub turned tail and ran back to its mother. These cubs had so much to learn in the few weeks before they would be out hunting with their parents. Every experience right now was new to them, and they would remember everything. Their survival depended upon it.

The cub that had been frightened by the leaf continued to watch it closely from the security of its mother's side. Suddenly the cub rushed forward, grabbed the leaf in its jaws, and shook its head so violently that it tumbled over. This was the tearing, killing bite that the older dogs use when they tackle real prey. Instinctively the cub knew what to do, but to whom it should do it and when and where would take much learning.

After a while, the six cubs started to play together. Two began rolling around in playful combat. The other four started what seemed to Ramu like a hunting game. The small cub with the torn ear was the prey. While one of his companions chased him, the others would jump at him and try to roll him over. It was funny to watch these cubs because, although they seemed to take their play seriously and appeared to know what they wanted to do, their wobbly bodies just wouldn't obey. A swift running attack would finish up in a nose dive. A playful bite, intended to be gentle, would be much too hard, and the companion would yelp and bite back angrily.

The smallest cub climbed back into the den and, to Ramu's surprise, came out dragging a piece of deerskin twice his length. Proudly he paraded with it, his little tail, not yet like a grownup's, stuck out like a defiant flag behind him.

Any time one of his littermates came near, he would growl at them. In spite of his size, they respected him. Eventually he allowed one of the cubs to seize the other end of the skin, and at once all the other cubs joined in a mighty tug-of-war. The tiny cub was dragged all over the place by the others, but he held on. Finally, the skin

shredded and broke and each cub had a piece to play with. They lost interest in the skin after that and grew tired. Their mother carried them back into the city, and Ramu, also feeling sleepy, crept quietly away.

9 Growing Up Fast

On his next visit a week later, Ramu learned even more about the wild dogs. The mother of the first litter of cubs was lying on her side in the shade opposite the den. One of the cubs wriggled over to her and started nursing. The other cubs heard their brother's loud, greedy sucking noises and immediately ran over to nurse. Very quickly the mother got up and growled at them. They all flattened down, with their half-grown ears pressed against their heads and their lips pulled back submissively. "Perhaps their sharp teeth are hurting her," Ramu wrote on his notepad. Then the cubs started to lick her face furiously, and she quickly threw up a few pieces of meat for them.

The other dogs, seeing the commotion around the mother, ran over to the cubs. Two of them gave what they had in their stomachs to the cubs when the greedy infants licked and nipped their mouths. *So they are being weaned,* Ramu observed. *And the other dogs help, too. What nice uncles they are.*

The dog that Ramu thought was their father then licked the hindquarters of each cub and he ate anything they passed, just as the mother did. Ramu now knew why the Wild Dog City was so clean. The adults eat the droppings of the infants and only pass their own droppings on the trail a long way from the den. Ramu recorded this conclusion in his notebook for the school report. *Wild dogs have found a solution to pollution and don't need a toilet at home,* he thought with amusement. But that would not be quite proper to include in his school report!

A couple of the cubs started growling and snapping at each other. One got hold of the other's cheek and shook it wildly. The other cub screamed and rolled over. They were testing each other. Over the next few weeks most of the cubs would have such a fight, and one would emerge as the leader. The fights would decide which cub dominated another, and this order would remain unchanged when the cubs became adults.

The adult chennai didn't intervene. They let the cubs go through this learning experience. But when the fight was over, their mother went over and sniffed and licked the two tusslers. Soon after, the cubs were playing together amicably.

The other cubs were discovering what fun it was to play with one of their uncles, probably much in the way they played in the den chamber with their mother. Two cubs were attacking the big dog's tail, which he switched from side to side to make the game more exciting. Another chewed on his ear and a fourth was repeatedly climbing onto the big dog's back and sliding down the far side. Then the uncle gave a short growl, stood up suddenly, walked away from the cubs, and lay down a few paces away. The one "killing" his ear had gone a little too far.

How gentle and understanding, Ramu reflected. *And what a simple way for the cub to learn that if it bites too hard, the game stops.*

The cubs were growing sleepy, and the shadows of the rocks and trees were growing long in the late afternoon sun. Their mother carried them, one by one, into the city, and the others left soon after to hunt.

Ramu hurried home, happy with such an exciting day and eager to tell his family about the cubs.

On each succeeding visit, he watched the cubs grow stronger and more confident. Altogether there were fourteen cubs, six from the first litter and four each from the two litters that came out of the den about a week after the first. The cubs were beginning to explore farther away from the city. They had four or five little "nursery" play areas in small clearings beneath the trees on the far bank of the nallah. This was almost at Ramu's eye level in the machan, and he had a good view of everything.

It was amazing, he thought, how the cubs seemed to be able to recognize their own mothers and littermates. By the time they were eight or nine weeks old, the cubs were all turning a sandy-brown color. Their ears were growing big and round. At this age their ears seemed too big for their heads.

The adults had started to bring back big pieces of their kills for the cubs to play with in the nursery, giving them a taste for the real thing. The first time the leader came in with a long deer leg, the cubs did not want to come near it. *What would happen when they saw their first whole live deer?* thought Ramu. *Would they run away?*

His favorite cub, with the torn ear, was the first to grab the leg. He seemed to thrive on this form of food and fun. Although Ramu had never seen him fight with any of the other cubs, he always seemed to get his own way and was catching up in size with the others. Ramu imagined that this cub might be a leader one day.

One week later, when the oldest litter was about ten weeks old, Ramu arrived at the machan. Only the two younger litters were out playing. The first litter was nowhere to be seen. Ramu waited anxiously all day for the cubs to appear. He couldn't imagine that a panther had killed them, since no panther in its right mind would go near a Wild Dog City. The chennai have been known to kill panthers and tigers, and none of the big cats are a match for the combined strength of a hungry pack. Perhaps part of the city had collapsed, trapping or crushing the mother and her cubs inside, while the others, out hunting, were not there to dig them out.

On and on Ramu fretted until late afternoon, when his spirits suddenly lifted. Down the nallah, tripping and wobbling over the rocks, came a string of cubs with their mother behind encouraging any stragglers. The rest of the pack brought up the rear. They had been out on their first hunting trip. The cubs, quite exhausted, collapsed on cool stones in the shade, with their legs stretched out, front and back.

None of them protested or even had the strength to wag a tail in response to the younger cubs, who ran around them exuberantly. They could smell that the cubs had already eaten, but no matter how much they persisted in licking their faces, their older cousins were too young and perhaps too greedy to part with any of the fine fare inside their distended stomachs.

A few days later, the younger cubs were taken out in separate hunting parties with their mothers and one or two of the adults. They spent less and less time around Wild Dog City, and some days they never returned to the dens. Ramu wondered where they might be. He asked Mr. David one Saturday evening.

10 A Crow to the Rescue

"They are probably hunting quite a few miles from the den now," said Mr. David knowledgeably. "The adults will leave the cubs—sometimes alone, sometimes with a babysitter—in some rocky or shrubby place. Here they can shelter from the heat and find refuge from any wild animal that could harm them. A serpent, an eagle, a leopard, and, of course, man, are their potential enemies."

He continued his lecture, rather formally, for he was proud and exact with his facts, most of which he had gathered himself over many years studying the chennai.

"Perhaps their worst enemy is their own friend-liness to our farm dogs. They may let some of them join the pack on a hunt and later die from distemper, that terrible disease that our dogs carry. Many cubs die from this some years. Other cubs starve in those years when there are too many of them and not enough deer. The farm cattle, which are too numerous, take much of the deer's food. No wonder the dogs take a few calves now and then. It's a wonder they don't take more. If the parents are not in the habit of killing calves, I think their cubs never will either."

Mr. David grew wistful, looking out of the cottage door into the far distance. Ramu read his silence as a kind of sadness for the way the jungle was being destroyed. His furrowed brow meant that he was still seeking a solution to help man and nature live together more harmoniously. Ramu felt very close to Mr. David just then.

"As the cubs get older, around three or four months, the pack take them on hunts rather than to the kill afterward," Mr. David continued. This is a dangerous time for the cubs. Some may get lost, fall and break one of their spindly legs, or be injured and killed by the deer. A deer with her fawn, provided she stands her ground and has her back against a rock, may repel a few dogs. I have seen two of the giant deer, the sambhur, stand back-to-back and keep several dogs away from their fawns. You will have great difficulty from now on trying to keep in contact with your cubs, since they will be hunting all over the east end of the valley. Sometimes several packs will have a reunion and hunt together for a while. Packs of twenty, and sometimes forty or more, chennai are not uncommon.

"In America, I hear they have little radios, called telemeters, which you attach on a collar on an animal that you have trapped. When you let it go, you just switch on your receiver and track it easily. Wouldn't it be nice to have some of those here?"

Ramu nodded in agreement, but he was feeling sad. He had no fancy radio thing to use, and the thought of never seeing his first family of cubs again made him downhearted. Mr. David laughed, and Ramu looked up in surprise. Surely Mr. David wasn't laughing at his unhappiness.

"Just think, Ramu. You don't need a telemeter to tell you where the cubs might be when their family has made a kill. Just think."

"Why, yes," exclaimed Ramu, after a moment's thought, "the jungle crows will tell me, and if they are near enough to me, I should be able to reach the cubs in time to see them for a while."

Late that afternoon, Sikka Bunda said, "Before the sun goes down, come to the river, my son. I have something to show you."

Ramu followed his father, knowing that he was to learn something important. On the way to the river, they saw two pi dogs gnawing on the fresh skull of a young domestic buffalo. Ramu's father approached them and they ran off a little way, afraid of a stranger. The dogs, and the remains of the buffalo, were from the neighboring patti. Sikka Bunda stuck the head high up in the fork of a tree, out of reach of the dogs.

"Poison?" inquired Ramu, and his father nodded. They walked on in silence toward an opening in the bamboo beside the river.

What Ramu saw made him stumble and almost fall into the water. Eight vultures lay dead, some in the water, others sprawled on the bank. Five or six vultures sat pathetically in the water, heads lowered, eyes closed, sipping water and then being sick. Ramu approached one. It looked at him, but was too weak to fly away. Half-opening its wings, it collapsed onto a rock. So majestic in the air, so pitiful now. Ramu felt his throat tighten, and he ran back to his father, who understood the hurt and the rage his son felt.

"Yes, Ramu, the innocent die when a farmer poisons the remains of a dead calf after a leopard or wild dogs have killed it. There are only twenty vultures to keep this part of the valley clean, and half of them—and who knows how many ravens— will be dead by morning."

They turned for home; the sun was setting over the Blue Hills. The bamboo and shrubs closed behind them as they left the river. Although everything looked the same as ever, Ramu would not forget; the anger that he felt gave way to pity for those poor birds and for the ignorant farmers who knew no better. Someday he would tell them, show them, help them to live in a better way with nature. Somehow he knew he would.

The next day Ramu took his pet crow, Baswey, with him. She was used to going on walks with him, sometimes riding on his shoulder, sometimes flying a few yards ahead and waiting in a tree until he caught up. When other crows started their *ca-caws,* she would point their direction and answer back, sometimes leaving Ramu for a while to join her kin to share the remains of a wild dog kill. He could usually tell by her direction and her distinctive

shrill call where the kill would be. But that day
he was unlucky.

Wednesday morning he went out again with
Baswey, and she located a kill that was only about
a half mile away. Ramu hurried as quickly as he
could between the thornbushes along the narrow
trail. Each bush seemed to reach out to hold him
back; the long spiny branches hooked his shirt,
even though he used his sharp aruval to clear a

way. Baswey seemed to understand that her friend wanted to accompany her, for instead of flying straight off, she flew a short way, stopped in a tree, and cawed and cawed until Ramu caught up, and then she flew on again. Perhaps she thought Ramu was hungry and was at last discovering something worth seeking in life!

As he approached the kill the air hummed with the sound of the vultures flying off. The chennai had already finished. *They can't be too far away,* he thought, and checking the direction of the wind, he decided to work around in a wide circle with the hopes of finding them at rest somewhere after their meal. Coming up over a small hill too quickly, he saw the dark tail and hind legs of a wild dog disappearing into the jungle. They had seen him and they would be off before he could watch them.

He kicked a rock, hard, with his toe, but it was not the pain that made him cry. He felt lost in a hopeless task. The chennai now moved too fast for him, even the cubs. The sunlight burst into bright stars as his eyes flooded with tears, and he sat down in the dust for a while and let his misery spill out. He watched an ant crawl over his sandal. *Was his foot over its trail?* he wondered. A rare flying squir-rel glided in front of him, between two wild mango trees. "If only I could fly," he wished. Looking up into the bright blue sky, he saw a tawny eagle drifting effortlessly on the warm rising air currents. He sniffed loudly, and as the things around gently drew him out of himself, he heard a mournful cry coming from a thick clump of bamboo near the river. He got up so quickly that Baswey lost two feathers flapping away in surprise. He stood very still and listened for the sound to come again so that he might fix its location more exactly. The cry came again and Ramu homed in on its source. He discovered a deep pit dug out many years before by local people mining for mica. Thick rotting stems of fallen bamboo covered the hole, from which came the sound of a little plaintive voice. Bending down into the hole, Ramu saw what the wild dogs had seen, but could not reach because of the fallen bamboo. A cub!

Swiftly he pushed aside the bamboo, hacking stubborn pieces with his aruval until he had space enough to climb down. The digging was only about six feet deep and the bamboo made an easy ladder for him. There, huddled in the corner of the pit, was a terrified cub. It grew silent as Ramu descended, and its lips curled defensively as his shadow swallowed it up. Ramu crouched as far from the cub as he could and sat quite still, talking to it now and then in a low, soothing voice. Slowly the cub calmed down and stopped snarling. Ramu tried extending a hand again. He crawled a little nearer and waited, then edged forward, inch by inch, closer and closer to the cub. With each slow inch, the cub seemed to lose its fear of him until it was within arm's reach. Then it simply crouched down, with its ears laid back, looking at him pathetically.

Very slowly and gently, he picked up the cub. It struggled briefly, but Ramu didn't fight it. He had handled animals before. He simply held it securely against his chest until the tense little body began to relax. Then he spoke to it gently again and gradually worked his way up the bamboo poles and out of the pit.

Talking in a reassuring voice and trying to disguise his elation, Ramu carried the cub home as fast as he could. By its torn left ear, he could tell that it was his favorite.

11 Ramu and Chennai

The cub pushed its head tightly under Ramu's arm and began to shiver again when Ramu's family crowded around to look at it.

"Isn't he a fine little fellow?" said Ramu. "He's the number one in the litter and I was lucky to save him."

"No," replied his father, "he is lucky that you saved him. But look, it's not a boy, but a girl!"

Ramu looked, with dismay. He had thought, because the cub was so plucky and outgoing, that it must be a boy.

"What are you going to call her?" asked Indhrani, grinning at her brother's mistake.

"Chennai, of course—what else?" he replied.

"But you can't keep her, Ramu," his mother said. "Where can you find meat for her?" That was a good question, indeed. "What little meat your father is given by the hunters he guides we need for ourselves."

"Go and see Mr. David," suggested Siddah. "He's staying at his bungalow for the week and he may be able to help. We will fix a bamboo enclosure for Chennai to stay in, but take her with you to Mr. David's so that he can look at her."

Ramu took the dirt road to Mr. David's place. It was only about two miles away. Mr. David was sitting on the verandah, cleaning out his guns.

"Why, Ramu, what a nice surprise, and what do you have there?"

Ramu showed him the cub, and after closing the verandah gate, they put Chennai on the floor. She froze on the spot, with her ears laid back and tail tucked tightly under her crouched legs. She was petrified.

"It's going to take a lot of time and patience to help her get over her fear. She is used to the wild and to her own kind. Let's try her with some fresh hare. I got two early this morning."

Chennai was too afraid to eat, but she sniffed the meat and showed a spark of interest in it.

"Once she settles, she will start to eat. You are lucky, Ramu. My freezer here has some hare and jungle fowl from last season, plus a few pieces of wild pork we haven't eaten. I'll give you the spare key and you can come and get meat whenever you need it. I'll be coming here often now because I want to finish writing my book of jungle tales. I'll be able to get some fresh meat once in a while for Chennai, too."

Ramu was relieved. The immediate future of his new companion was now secure.

"What about that disease she can get from our pi dogs?" he suddenly asked.

"We must go to the animal refuge and get your animal vaccinated," Mr. David said.

Half an hour later they drove up to the animal refuge, where homeless cats, worn-out donkeys and mules and oxen lazed around. The animal attendant showed them a fawn they had rescued from a pack of wild dogs. The fawn had actually run into the shelter compound as though to seek help from the people there!

Mr. David took Ramu and Chennai into the dispensary, and the old Englishman who was in charge scowled at the cub and gruffly exclaimed,

"A wild dog cub! All wild dogs should be shot; they ruin the deer for hunters and kill dozens of helpless fawns. They are born killers. They just kill for pleasure."

Ramu felt a rush of anger—he hadn't expected such words from an animal lover. Then he came back with a reply that silenced the man and pleased and surprised Mr. David.

"The chennai have been hunting deer for thousands of years before any people were here, so if they are such murderers, then why aren't all the deer gone? The wild dogs keep the herds healthy by removing the surplus fawns and the less-fit adults."

The crusty Englishman, taking a closer look at the cub, felt a slight compassion for the little creature. His face softened and he said, "I will give you some pills for worms and some flea powder." After examining the cub, he declared her to be healthy but in need of plenty of fresh meat since she had a lot of growing to do. "You might add a little rice and vegetable scraps, too, so as to make it a more balanced diet. Bring her back in about a month for her booster vaccination."

Ramu winced as the man gave Chennai her

first shot, and, to their surprise she uttered a low growl. "Feisty little mite—just keep her away from your people's calves," said the man.

Mr. David drove Ramu and Chennai to their cottage. The bamboo enclosure was ready when they arrived. The edges of the enclosure were lined with split trunks of bamboo so that the cub couldn't dig her way out. A box in one corner would provide her shade and a sense of security. She ran straight inside it, and Ramu left meat and water for her by the entrance to her "den."

"You realize, Ramu," reflected Mr. David, "that the chances of the pack coming here are pretty slim, even if she calls to them tonight. They have probably given her up, and even if you set her free, it would be one chance in a thousand that they would ever find her."

Ramu felt relieved because he was feeling a twinge of guilt about keeping a wild animal in captivity. The bamboo enclosure did look like a prison. And, like a prison warden, the family's pi dog, Jimmy, kept circling the enclosure, his tail up high with excitement. Tomorrow Ramu would introduce the two; the cub had been through enough for one day.

Ramu was simply too charged-up to sleep that

night. The cub couldn't sleep either—but for a different reason. It was crying for its family in loud whines and *oo oo* howls. This went on until the early hours of the morning, when suddenly it stopped. Ramu felt uneasy and went to see if the cub was asleep. Sudden silence could mean danger. As he went outside, he heard a deep snarl and something dark and large ran off into the shadows. A panther or black leopard! Was it just curious about the cub or was it going to kill her? The next day they would have to fix some kind of roof on the enclosure to keep that unwelcome visitor away. Ramu decided that the safest thing was to take the cub indoors for the remainder of the night.

Soon they were both snuggled up together. Chennai obviously enjoyed the security of Ramu's warm tummy. In no time they were both fast asleep.

Ramu wasn't sure which of them woke first, but the cub was still by his side when Ramu woke. He sat up and Chennai looked at him and then scooted down under the blanket to the bottom of the bed and hid there. So Ramu lay down and kept quite still, calling to the cub in a soft voice.

Indhrani woke up, heard him, and exclaimed, "Are you talking in your sleep or do you really have that cub in bed with you?"

Ramu explained to her in whispers what had happened the previous night, and then he asked her to bring some of the leftover meat from the enclosure.

With this, Ramu soon coaxed Chennai to him, and she hungrily gobbled the meat from his hand. Then, when she licked his fingers afterward and kept on doing so, he knew that it wasn't just the taste of meat she liked. She was grateful.

Indhrani took a note to school to explain Ramu's absence, for it was a very special day indeed. Ramu had to win the confidence of Chennai and she had to learn to trust him. By evening he was tired, but at least whenever he approached the cub she no longer cringed; instead, Chennai just sat there and occasionally gave him a lick or a push with her nose.

Every time Ramu gave her a piece of meat, he would call her name, and she quickly learned to come when called. After a couple of days she was following him around the enclosure. Ramu had to introduce Jimmy, since the two dogs would meet sooner or later.

The little cub greeted the big pi dog like a long-lost friend, whining, licking, and rolling over in a frenzy of released loneliness for her own kind. Jimmy stood quite still, looking a little nonplussed

by this shower of affection from an unknown distant cousin.

Ramu joined them in the enclosure and patted Jimmy so that he wouldn't feel jealous. Jimmy gave him a cursory lick and briefly wagged his tail. This acted like a magnet on the cub; she greeted Ramu just as she had Jimmy.

12 Wild and Tame

Jimmy and Ramu became Chennai's pack mates, and the three of them would go exploring together. Baswey often accompanied them. The crow seemed to have a special liking for the cub whom she would tease by repeatedly hopping up very close and then flying off as Chennai tried to catch her. Chennai always stayed close to Ramu and never went off alone.

On these outings Ramu learned a lot from Jimmy and Chennai, as he discovered how they found things. Although they used their sense of sight and hearing, as he did, their sense of smell gave them an extra advantage. Over rocky areas, Ramu's eyesight was of little use. Because there was no dust in these areas, there was no record of animal tracks. The dogs' superb sense of smell enabled them to follow scent trails over the rocks. They preferred to move with the wind in their faces so that they could smell anything in the air that might mean excitement ahead.

Going off with Chennai let Ramu into her world, and he gradually came to understand how the world must seem to her. She could detect the slightest sound or movement, and her sense of smell was far better than Jimmy's. Or was she just much quicker to react? With one bound she could catch a hare completely unaware after stalking it some distance, and she could even leap fast and high enough to grab a quail or partridge in midflight.

Whenever the trio came to one of the communal areas where other wild dogs deposited their droppings, Chennai would get very aroused and sniff everything. Jimmy showed little interest and sat there looking indifferent, if not actually bored. Surely Chennai was remembering her own kind and perhaps even recognizing, vaguely, some familiar smells from her own family.

Chennai got into trouble one day, in spite of her

remarkable abilities. She was so intent on following a trail with her nose that she didn't bother to look up as she went behind a rock. Ramu yelled a warning, for he saw the black and yellow glint of a sleeping porcupine. Too late. The eager chennai cub went head first into the porcupine and came back yelping with pain. Luckily, the few quills were in her head. They had missed her eyes by a fraction. Chennai crowded into a dense growth of shrubs and whined; she growled when Ramu tried to approach. She was frightened.

Ramu's soothing voice calmed her and she understood that he meant to help. "One, two, three, and one more," said Ramu as he pulled out the quills. Chennai yelped and grabbed his hand in her mouth, biting gently. "That's it, Chennai," said Ramu, as he patted her reassuringly. She licked his face and was off, racing in a wild circle around Jimmy as though to let off steam after the grueling experience.

On their travels Chennai discovered all kinds of things: a snake's molted skin, a tortoiseshell, a leopard's skull with beautiful fangs for Ramu's collection, and someone's lost hunting knife. She had an uncanny knack for finding giant monitor lizards and long rat snakes that were hiding. Somehow they never clashed with a cobra or a Russel's viper, which was surprising since Chennai put her nose into everything. Chennai's best "find" was a cleanly washed pair of man's trousers. She came running up to Ramu proudly, with the pants trailing from her jaws. *How did she get hold of those?* Ramu wondered. Then suddenly he guessed how and quickly went down to the river where the women were doing their laundry. He held up the trousers and apologized profusely to the woman who claimed them. She was amused and jokingly suggested that Chennai keep them so she wouldn't have to iron them.

Although the cattle owners grew more and more alarmed when they saw how big and strong Chennai was becoming, they had no cause for alarm. Perhaps because she was being raised surrounded by cattle and calves, she never regarded them as a potential meal. The farmers were amazed and reassured when they saw Chennai walk quietly through a dozen or more calves standing in the shade. Even though she got on well with the calves, some of the older cattle, who must have encountered wild dogs before, would lower their heads and threaten Chennai if she came near. She always kept well away from these characters. Her worst enemy was the large bull buffalo who nearly gored her one day while she was sleeping near the cottage. But for Jimmy, who barked a warning and gallantly bit the bull's heels to distract him, she might have been killed. After that experience, Chennai chose to sleep in the safest place during the day—on the flat bamboo roof over her enclosure!

At night Ramu put Chennai in the bamboo enclosure for safety, but during the day, when he was at school, she had the free run of the place. He had wanted to take her to school and show her off, but she was shy of strangers, even of Mr. David who visited often, bringing fresh meat. She accepted only Ramu and Indhrani and Jimmy. This fear of strangers would later help save her life.

After Ramu let Chennai loose early one morning, she and Jimmy disappeared. They had done this before and Ramu wanted to know just what they were up to.

Baswey started ca-cawing and pointing with her head at two other ravens in a tree high up on the hillside. Ramu and Baswey went to investigate.

There, in a gully, was Jimmy, Chennai, and a big wild dog he had never seen before, all eating a fawn they had just killed. "So that's why Chennai hasn't been eating all the meat I gave her," Ramu said to himself. "How good it is that she can get her own food." But for her love for Jimmy and Ramu and his sister, she might have returned to the wild from then on. Jimmy was an expert hunter and must have taught her a few tricks. Ramu wondered where the wild dog came from. It was too old to be Chennai's brother. Perhaps it was a grown male looking for a mate of its own.

Ramu approached the trio and with his aruval cut off a good piece of meat for his family. "Look," he proudly proclaimed when he got home, "Chennai is now feeding us." His parents enjoyed the fresh roast venison that night. It was a rare treat.

The next morning a jeep pulled up in the yard with a forest official and two angry-looking farmers.

"You have a wild dog here, don't you?" asked the uniformed officer. He had a thick black toothbrush mustache, which made his white teeth look even brighter, and a permanent smile on his shiny face.

Ramu told him that he had.

"It has killed three of these farmers' calves. Your animal will have to be shot," the officer said.

Old Siddah came out of the cottage and quickly appraised the situation. He saw the gun between the divided front seat of the jeep, and he knew the two farmers from the neighboring patti. They would do anything to kill wild dogs and they often used poison. He also knew that they kept too many cattle for the yield of their grazing land. Their calves probably starved to death and were then eaten by hungry farm dogs.

"So when were these calves killed?" old Siddah asked. With hesitation, the farmers replied, "Last night, and that's not the first time."

"That's not fair," cried Ramu. "I shut Chennai up every night in the enclosure. It couldn't have been her."

The forest official lost his smile and looked sternly at the farmers. He didn't like wild dogs and was all for poisoning them, but he didn't like to look stupid and go off on wild goose chases.

"Next time, be sure of your facts," the officer said, and he roared off in the jeep, leaving the dejected farmers to walk home by themselves.

Ramu invited them to see his wild dog and to watch her with the calves, but they shook their heads and muttered, "The only good wild dog is a skinned one" and "Give me her head and I'll get twenty rupees bounty on the killer."

Ramu watched them leave, but fear and anger remained inside him long after they disappeared from view.

"Some people," said Siddah with a shrug, "have less sense than animals and do much more harm than the meanest tusker. Beware of the man with the smile. He doesn't like to lose or to be made a fool of. He will be back again."

Ramu gave his report to the class a few days later and told them about the problem with the farmers. Everyone agreed that the chennai had a bad name with people and that they had as much right to live as any other creature. But no one could find a solution for peace. The teacher suggested that Ramu spend some time reading the journals and books on conservation and wildlife management that Mr. David kept in his extensive library at the bungalow. Ramu accepted this assignment with pleasure because he knew that Mr. David was one of the few people involved in trying to save the chennai.

"What's the most important thing in favor of keeping the chennai in the jungle?" his teacher asked before the class broke up for the long summer vacation.

Several hands were raised and a few students

repeated the important things that Ramu had told them, that they kept the deer herds healthy and that they were very intelligent, loving, and had a highly developed family life.

"What else?" prodded the teacher. Even Ramu was silent and stuck for an answer.

"Why, there's no other predator left in the valley except for the occasional panther or leopard," said the teacher. "All the tigers are gone, which makes the preservation of the chennai even more vital. Without them, the balance of nature in our valley would be destroyed forever."

What a good point, thought Ramu. This was perhaps the strongest defense in favor of the wild dogs.

As he ran home, he wondered what adventures he and Chennai would have during the long summer. Then, like a black cloud, the thought of the forest official came into his mind. Ramu wished that he would never see that man again. Perhaps old Siddah was wrong this time. But he never was, as a rule.

13 Summer Adventures

One bright moonlit night in late June, Ramu and Chennai set out to see inhabitants of the jungle that don't show themselves during the day. As they walked along the trail near his house, a nightjar made them jump. This strange night-flying bird was lying on the trail in front of them, confident they could not see it because of its camouflaged colors. Just before Ramu stepped on it, the bird flew up in his face without a sound. The white marks on its unfolded wings flashed like luminous beacons. Ramu hoped that all of the night animals wouldn't scare him that way.

During the day the shadows of the trees over

the rocks and water seemed to stroke and cool them like gentle hands. But by moonlight these same shadows came alive and Ramu saw incredible beasts that forever writhed and changed their form and character. The wind rustled through the trees, coming closer and closer like a great mammoth of the night. When it hit the bamboo near the river, it groaned and creaked, and Ramu heard the unearthly music of the wind playing on the holes in the bamboo. He knew these sounds by day, but at night they had an awesome and magical quality about them.

The night-prowling tiger's roar no longer echoed in the jungle, and its sound, which symbolized everything that is wild and free, was only a memory to Ramu. But the elephant endured and the distant sound of one ripping bamboo to eat was like someone setting off firecrackers at a village temple festival.

On the riverbank they could hardly hear the rushing water for the sound of frogs. Every stone seemed to be croaking its own tune because the frogs were hiding underneath them. All the frogs stopped croaking as Ramu stepped onto one of the stones. He sat with Chennai waiting patiently on a large boulder in the middle of the stream. Slowly the stones seemed to come back to life until the two of them were swallowed up in an undulating torrent of sound. Bats flew silently above them in the narrow clearing between the bamboo, darting and twisting at high speed to snatch up flying insects. How different the stream was at night.

They sat there for a long time, letting the different sounds and smells of the night world ebb and flow around them. A barking deer called from the jungle, and a couple of scavenging jackals yipped and yodeled. They had probably just feasted on someone else's leftovers—or caught a hare themselves. Three other jackals called in higher voices from deeper in the jungle. No doubt their nearly full-grown cubs were out scavenging for themselves in preparation for their independent life as adults. Unlike their chennai cousins, jackals do not form packs or make cities.

Chennai suddenly tensed and Ramu followed the direction of her gaze. A large porcupine had come to drink and was delicately sipping from the river only a few feet away. It continued drinking slowly and rhythmically, even when a peacock gave its weird catlike call from the shadows close by. Nothing disturbs the armored porcupine except an animal encroaching on its territory.

After a while Ramu called Chennai and they set off for home. As they passed under a grove of overhanging mango trees, Chennai hung back to sniff the fresh tracks of a sloth bear. Suddenly the overhanging branches exploded and a black panther stood directly in front of Ramu, blocking his path. It hissed and spat at him. Its fangs flashed menacingly in the moonlight. Two golden eyes burned into Ramu who stood frozen like a statue, ready

to swing his aruval. It was probably the same panther he had chased away from Chennai that first
night, and he was sure the animal remembered
him.

The panther tensed, ready to leap, but something
brushed past Ramu and leaped at the panther. It
was Chennai in a silent fury that Ramu had never
thought her capable of. The big cat was taken off-
guard. It checked its leap, twisted sideways and

scrambled into the nearest tree. A muffled growl came from its throat. It had been chased before by wild dogs and feared them. For the panther, one chennai meant many, and it was sure that there was a whole pack nearby. Chennai growled and barked and jumped up at the high refuge where the scared cat was clinging, then followed Ramu home. She had saved her friend's life that night.

Although Ramu was never swift enough to follow Chennai on her early morning hunts with the two dogs, he sometimes saw them bring down a deer. That large red male wild dog was always with them, and Ramu wondered if Chennai would mate with him. Perhaps her attraction to this wild dog would become stronger as she matured and she would eventually leave forever. Ramu felt a twinge of jealousy, but he knew deep inside that Chennai would not stay with him forever.

The long summer days hummed slowly by, and the dry earth shimmered in the heat. Soon the rains would come and all would be green again, the deer would have their fawns, and Ramu would be back at school. How quickly the summer vacation passed. When he wasn't out with Chennai or doing chores, Ramu was buried deep in the books and articles Mr. David had loaned him. Mr. David was writing

113

a proposal that he would present to the governor of the state and to the chief of the forest service. In it was a sound policy to protect not only the chennai, but also the farmers in the whole valley. Ramu read it with interest, although he had difficulty with some of the legal terms.

"There will be incredible pressure against my proposal at all levels," said Mr. David. "If I can get the hunters on my side and the bounty on the chennai removed, we have won the first step."

"Why do you want the hunters on your side, Mr. David?"

"Because when I prove to them that the deer are healthier and have better prize stags in the herds when the chennai are there, they will be all for saving our friends. Also we have to outlaw poisoning and give all the wild animals a much larger sanctuary to live in. Many of the wild dogs have part of their hunting range in the protected sanctuary here and the rest on land where they can be shot. They need more protected space. Hunting will be allowed only in the areas where there are farms. A few farms will have to be relocated, but this would be no hardship for the farmers since the land would be free. As it is now, they pay the forest department a small fee for permission to graze their cattle in the jungle during the day. In so doing, the cattle eat up much of what should be allotted to the deer and other wild animals. This, too, we will have to put a stop to. The worst crime they commit is to burn off large areas of the jungle to make it into grazing land for their stock. The habitat of the jungle animals is then ruined."

Ramu felt dizzy with all these things that had to be done to save the chennai. It was no simple problem, and the solution was not simple either.

Something happened a few mornings later to save Chennai, at least on the home front. While walking on a trail that passed by the neighboring patti, Chennai spotted a herd of wild pigs in a potato field. They had broken through the bamboo and thornbush barricade and were ruining the crop. While Chennai chased the pigs from the field, Ramu ran to the nearest cottage and aroused the owner. It was one of the farmers who wanted Chennai shot.

"Well, why tell me before you have chased the pigs off my potatoes first," he cried ungratefully.

Then, when the farmer saw how swiftly Chennai had evicted the pigs, he couldn't help feeling a little grateful. He said nothing, but gave Ramu an armload of fresh potatoes. Ramu saw a slight gleam of admiration for Chennai in the man's eyes. She had won over an enemy at last.

14 Smugglers!

Plodding along one of the dirt roads in the jungle on their way home one evening, Ramu heard the sound of someone chopping wood a little farther up the road. The sun was setting over the hills, which were turning blue and purple, and the blue sky was streaked with pink and gold. The breeze was cool and felt good on his face. Chennai picked up the scent of something interesting, for she suddenly vanished into the bushes.

Coming round the bend, Ramu stopped in surprise. There were three men, complete strangers, stowing pieces of brown wood into a battered old car and a fourth was splitting logs and hacking out the center portion. Sandalwood smugglers! Before he could hide, two of the men saw him. "How many more of you are there?" one of the smugglers demanded, as he pulled a shotgun out of the car. Ramu had heard that these men would shoot to kill because the penalties for stealing sandalwood were severe.

Ramu told them that there were no other people with him. They made him stand by the hacked tree stump and ordered him to wait until they had packed up and driven away. If he called for help, he knew that he might never shout again. He was also aware that it would soon be dark and that this part of the jungle was a dangerous place where leopards roamed and the man-killing crossed tusker was last seen.

When the men weren't looking, he gave three low whistles, the rallying call for Chennai.

"What was that?" asked one of the men, looking suspiciously at Ramu.

"Oh, some bird," said another. "Hurry up and get this stuff loaded."

Chennai heard the call and came silently toward the group. Ramu's tense body conveyed that he was in trouble and Chennai growled and bared her fangs threateningly at the men. They didn't know that she was too afraid to actually attack them.

"Wild dogs," they cried, and like the panther, expecting a whole pack to surround them, they scrambled into their car.

"What about the boy?" asked one of them.

"Let him look out for himself," said the driver, as he gunned the engine and raced off—much too quickly for that kind of road. They hit a large boulder, skidded, and piled into the ditch alongside the dirt road.

Before they came to their senses, Ramu was racing down the road with Chennai to the checkpoint about two miles away. There would be a telephone at the gate house. The surprised gate man called up the forest department office immediately. The sandalwood smugglers surrendered readily. With a smashed car, they had no way to escape, and they preferred prison to a night alone in the jungle.

15 Return to the Wild

The news soon spread that Ramu and Chennai had caught a band of thieves, and the valley people were all talking about it. The story grew, as stories will, until it went that Ramu had caught twenty smugglers by calling up all the wild dogs to attack them, and an elephant had smashed their car.

The many versions of the story eventually reached Madras, and a newspaper reporter was sent down to investigate the rumors. By the end of the summer, Chennai was the local hero and even had her photograph published in *The Hindu,* a national newspaper. Mr. David was glad of this because it put in a good word for the wild dog. Also, the reporter who visited the valley to get the story, gave a page to describe Mr. David's conservation program. It was sure to reach a wide and influential audience.

The first day of school was a letdown. Ramu knew that he could spend less time with Chennai during the week, but it was good to be at school and feel so important after having been written up in the newspaper.

His glory was short-lived. That evening the forest official with the smiling face drove up in his jeep, blowing his horn loudly as he approached the cottage.

The first thing he did was to ask for Ramu. Ramu stepped forward; his knees were shaking and he had a sour taste on his tongue. His family stood behind him, but Ramu knew it would be different this time.

The forest officer smiled and said, "Show me your permit for owning a chennai. It's forest government property you know."

Ramu said he had no permit and asked how he could get one.

"How can I get one?" he insisted, with a note of hurt and anger in his voice.

121

"By applying to the main office, but it is unlikely that you will get one since the chennai are regarded as vermin, to be destroyed by gun, poison, or any other means possible. And if you did get a license, your varmint would have to be caged permanently and never allowed to run free."

The uniformed man's teeth shone in the moonlight as he made his pronouncement.

"With no license, you must give the animal to a zoo under my stamp of approval or have it shot by tomorrow evening."

Ramu's father came forward then and asked the pompous fellow why he liked to make trouble. The official's smile froze and he replied that he was only following regulations.

Old Siddah strode right up to him and simply looked him in the eyes. The officer looked away and Siddah said, "A man who looks away is less than an animal, for he lies. He does not believe in his heart what his head tells him. You feed on rules and regulations. I am sorry for your children."

This was the worst possible insult, and it cut deeply into the man's façade. His eyes bulged a little and beads of sweat appeared on his face. Siddah had demolished him and, like a mirror, had shown the man just what he was.

The officer coughed loudly and, avoiding Siddah's eyes, addressed Ramu.

"Remember, you have until tomorrow night." And without daring to look at anyone else, he drove off in a cloud of dust.

Ramu was too angry to cry. He discussed with his family what he should do, and all agreed that the only thing to do was to take Chennai far out into the jungle and leave her. Ramu decided he would leave her at Wild Dog City where she had been born. He would borrow his father's shotgun to scare her away if she tried to follow him. He hoped she would meet up with her kin and live in peace.

Everyone was up early the next morning to say good-bye, including Ramu's relatives who kept their cattle in the adjoining patti. They all loved and respected Chennai.

The boy and the wild dog set off together over the hill, and the people watched them walk into the rising sun. Some wondered if Ramu would return. The two seemed so close to each other and to nature.

Chennai again sensed something in Ramu's mood. She kept nuzzling him as he walked along. Ramu could not see the trail very well because his eyes were tired and swollen from a sleepless night of tears.

They reached Wild Dog City after an hour or so and sat down together. Ramu spoke softly to Chennai. Although she did not understand his words, she seemed to know what he felt and what was happening by the tone of his voice. She sat close to him, her big ears alert and twitching now and then. A light breeze ruffled her glossy coat, but she didn't turn in its direction, as was her habit, to test it with her nose. Her eyes never left his face.

Ramu looked into her face for what he thought was the last time and said, "Chennai, remember some of us are your friends, but trust no man. You are on your own now and you must never return to me. Thank you for being my friend." He stood up quickly, closed his eyes and fired the gun. The sound echoed in the nallah. The shot peppered the trees above Chennai's head. She simply sat there looking at him, with her ears back and a soft look in her eyes.

Ramu walked away, not daring to look back in case Chennai saw the hurt in his eyes and his longing for her to stay with him. He did not look back until he reached the turn in the trail on the ridge of the hill that led down into the valley.

Nearing home, he sat on a rock and looked down into the valley. It was early afternoon. His eyes scanned the patchwork quilt of greens and browns and traced the rivers running under brighter threads of green and gold. How peaceful it seemed from here. In his mind's eye he saw the cautious deer going to drink and hesitating at the water's edge, always suspicious of danger and ready to flee; the elephant, like a statue, so large but so quiet, standing in bamboo shade; a noisy troop of monkeys cavorting through the treetops in search of food; peacocks parading and pecking under the trees; a procession of ants briskly foraging under and over the stones and dry leaves; a farmer calling his cattle and another playing with his children; and the women carrying water and gathering firewood before preparing the evening meal.

For a moment, time seemed to stop for him and he was able to see everything in the valley coming together as one. How simple, he reflected. Although every tree, every animal, and every person is different and separate, they are all one. He felt an overwhelming sense of peace and a new strength filled his body. Siddah's words echoed in his ears. "A man must work for peace if he feels it in his heart."

126

His own voice replied to the jungle below, *I will help you all, yes, I will.*

He did not know the words to express further what he was feeling, but he knew what it was to be a man and to have found a cause to work for. He stepped down the hillside with his head high and his father met him on the way. Both understood. There was nothing more to be said. Ramu took his father's hand and they went home.

About the Author

Dr. Michael Fox went to India last year to observe the wild dog, to draw public attention to its plight, and to make recommendations which would help ensure its future survival in the natural habitat.

The author is a noted authority on animal behavior, combining the background of a degree from London's Royal Veterinary School and a PhD in psychology from London University with a profound concern for the well-being and conservation of wildlife. His unique perception and his affection for animals is apparent in such books as *Vixie: The Story of a Little Fox,* the Christopher Award winning *The Wolf,* and *Sundance Coyote.* These books are largely based on firsthand observation: Dr. Fox has personally raised coyotes, red, gray, and arctic foxes, timber wolves and jackals—as well as dogs and cats.

A professor of psychology at Washington University, Dr. Fox makes his home in St. Louis, Missouri. This fall he will return to India to resume his work on behalf of the wild dog.

About the Artist

An enthusiastic amateur archaeologist, Michael Hampshire has spent the last two years working on *The Emergence of Man* series, a project ideally suited to his interests, which called for extensive travel to Mediterranean countries and throughout Europe.

Michael Hampshire spent a summer in India, and the authenticity and feeling for the country shown in his illustrations for *A Cow for Jaya* have been widely praised.

When he isn't traveling, Mr. Hampshire lives in New York City.